Ian
and the Great Silver Dragon:
A Friendship Begins

IAN

AND
THE

GREAT SILVER DRAGON:
A FRIENDSHIP BEGINS

JIM DILYARD

THE WOOSTER BOOK COMPANY

Wooster Ohio • 2016

The Wooster Book Company

205 West Liberty Street
Wooster, Ohio 44691

www.woosterbook.com

Printed and bound in the United States of America.

Cover and text illustrations by Amy Rottinger.

ISBN: 978-1-59098-646-2

∞ This book is printed on acid-free paper comprising at least 50% post-consumer recycled fiber.

Dedication:

to all the SEEKERS *who realized
that this story should continue,
and so it shall.*

Contents

Acknowledgements

I want to thank all of you who have had the courage and curiosity to read the first book in this series. Special thanks go out to Diane and Sharda for their endless support and editing skills and ideas. I greatly value their wisdom and insight. Amy has once again created artistic mastery. This book is a collaboration of several people, places, and events from my past and the relationships of the present. The ideas and story would not be here if it were not for your unselfish contributions. I will always be in humble debt to each of you.

Introduction

Welcome readers to the second story of Ian and his new friend, the Great Silver Dragon. Our journey started in the first book of this series and now it is time to start a new adventure.

Ian had questions on his first encounter with Bry-Ankh and now is ready to ask and seek more. In Book One, we laid down the foundation for the steps to greater knowledge. The energies of the universe were discussed and the beginnings of the recipe for success were established. The ideas of BE, DO, and HAVE were brought to your attention as well as the idea of focused thinking which is necessary for dreams to come true.

Ian wants more from his encounter with the Great Silver Dragon. His imagination has been ignited. He seeks many things, but at the top of the list is a friend, a true friend that will listen to him, support him, and love him for all that he is. He wonders if Bry-Ankh, or just plain Bry, as he is about to learn, can fill the desires of his heart.

The reader will discover these answers together with Ian and his new friend as they travel to far away and distant places that are back in the time of the great kingdoms of the Old World. There is mystery, magic, and power to open the door to other dimensions, which are just a few pages, or lifetimes away.

Can the past help you in this moment? Will it allow you to see this time period and the future in a new way? Only you, the reader, can answer. Are you not now just a little curious?

Chapter One
A Dragon Returns

A WONDERFUL SUMMER EVENING is unfolding at the estate. Ian's brother and a group of his friends are out at the pool. Music is playing rather loudly but you can still hear laughter and splashing as they jump in and out of the water. A poolside basketball hoop is getting a lot of attention. The game is not about putting the ball in the hoop but about mugging the person attempting to make a shot. Food is being consumed at an alarming rate which is the normal procedure when the pool is in use. Summer evenings are perfect for this type of relaxation, unless you have a dragon for a friend.

Ian is out in the courtyard away from the pool. He has the two shop cats, Squeak and W-L with him. They are on patrol looking for anything that is smaller than they are and makes the mistake of moving. Cats are constant observers and always on guard for the possibility of a mouse invasion. Ian enjoys watching the swishing tails and the crouch of the hunt which is followed by a leap of death towards some unsuspecting prey.

Either cat at any time may give up the hunt and decide to rub around Ian's legs. Or roll on their back asking for a tummy rub. This evening they are interested in personal attention. Ian is setting on a large warm stepping stone with his back to the flowers and the cats are getting their heads scratched between their ears. Once in a while, one of them will roll over wanting a tummy rub which is followed by loud and excessive purring.

Squeak was brought home by Ian's father who found him hungry and homeless at one of his oil well sites. Squeak was just a little kitten with a small cut above one eye and a very high-pitched voice. That is how he got his name. His white and orange fur looks like pieces of a jig-saw puzzle.

W-L on the other hand just showed up one morning by the kitchen door. She also had a hungry and homeless look and was very small herself and starving for food. Her coat is classic tortoise shell with a distinctive grey and black color. She made up for her prior lack of nourishment and became a large and healthy consumer of food, which helped her become a slightly portly cat earning her the nickname "W-L" which stands for Wide Load. Not a very endearing nickname, but one that fits her personality.

Everyone is having a wonderful time and Ian is feeling good about the companionship and the attention factor from his furry friends. His relaxation has allowed his mind to roam and he turns his thoughts to dragons.

Ian has had much to think about from his experience with Bry-Ankh. He remembers that Bry-Ankh told him that he could call him by his first name, Bry. All Ian needs to do is become calm and concentrate on seeing his friend, the Great Silver Dragon, and Bry will come to him. He decides to try and see if Bry will appear.

Ian closes his eyes and slows his breathing down and just thinks about Bry. At first nothing happens and Ian is starting to get a little concerned and wonders if he is doing the invitation correctly. He hears the cats purring and feels them on his lap and against a leg to get his attention. He then notices the smell of the air has changed to that of a warm spring rain. This he remembers—could it be that his friend is nearby? There is a quick, bright flash of light in Ian's closed eyes and the ground shakes with a vibration of something heavy, softly hitting it. It is then that Ian knows Bry is there.

Ian slowly opens his eyes and, yes, there before him is Bry, the Great Silver Dragon. What is interesting is that the furry friends, Squeak and W-L, don't seem to be startled by Bry at all. In fact both of them walk over to this very large and bright dragon, rub up against one of his massive legs, and purr ever so loudly. "Greetings to you, fine Ian, and your companions," Ian hears Bry say, and he notices the loving smile from Bry that always seems to make him relax and breathe normally. "Thank you, Bry," he replies and with that, Bry bows and lowers his head in a sign of respect. "How may I be of service to you today?" he asks.

Ian replies, "I want to learn more about what you know and how things really work."

Bry does not respond immediately. He just looks at Ian for a short moment and his brilliant red eyes shine like rubies in the sunlight. "Ian," Bry says, "what you asked for I can do, but doing so will take time and you must be willing to make a commitment to do and to study what I teach you. Are you willing, and will you try to believe, even if it seems that what I say you may not understand when I first say it to you?"

Ian thinks that this is a strange way of answering his question but he believes in Bry, so he says, "Yes."

Chapter Two
A Face to Face Discussion

BRY LETS OUT A LONG SLOW BREATH of his own and settles down in front of Ian. His great tail curls around his feet. He looks at Ian and asks, "Ian, would it be easier for you if my size or shape is different so that our conversations would be more like what you are used to at school?"

Ian is happy to hear this because the great size of Bry does bother him a little and he feels a bit ill at ease when talking with Bry and so he answers, "Oh please, yes."

A small quick flash of light makes Ian blink his eyes and Bry shrinks in size and stature to one equal to that of Ian. Ian is thrilled with this because now they both can see eye to eye with each other. Bry looks at Ian and asks "Are you ready, my apprentice?"

Ian responds, "Yes," even before Bry is finished.

"Good," says Bry, "because we have already started. This is our first lesson and it started with you making an agreement with me to become a student, to listen to what I tell you, and to take time to study and observe what is being said. It is of utmost importance that when you make an agreement with someone, or dragon, that you do everything in your power to keep it. By keeping agreements, you build and define your character and strengthen your resolve to proper action. You must believe and listen to your teacher and have trust that the information you are getting is honest and real. Once you have established this trust, you can then start the process of learning

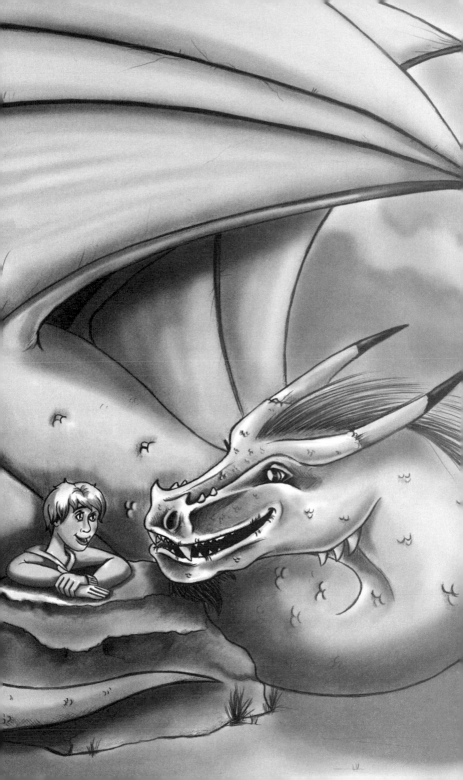

and believing. The *process of believing* is different from just believing. The process part contains action steps which need to be taken in order to establish the depth and strength of believing. Do you have any questions yet young one?" Ian shakes his head "no," so Bry continues.

"The first part of your desire to learn is to decide who do you listen to. This may sound like a simple question, but it is not. The person, or dragon, speaking to you must be believable. The question is how to decide if they are. It is best to take advice from someone who has the qualities you want or who has been where you want to go. The only way to establish this is to observe what is happening and to ask questions. You must never be afraid of asking a question. Then listen closely to the answer and have an awareness of how the answer makes you feel."

"Take our relationship as an example. Why should you trust and believe in me? I am a dragon and that is enough to cause you to be nervous and skeptical. My information seems to sound good and you will find out it works. But how do you know? The answer, again, is to check with your feelings. Take time to examine how you feel, and if the feeling is good, then this is someone you should put your trust in. Your feelings and emotions are your internal guidance system and your truth detectors. Observing and trusting in your feelings will get easier as you practice them. When the feelings are good, the results will usually be good."

Bry pauses to let what he has said have time to find a place in Ian's memory. He studies his student's body language and waits to see if he understands. He sees that Ian is not showing any signs of confusion, so he continues.

"There is a formula for learning and it starts with learning the basics. We dragons have a saying that a basic lesson can take a short time to learn and a lifetime to master. We are always on the path of being masters as it is a goal that we are reaching for. Mastery of something is not a place but a journey and the number one goal of the journey is to feel good about everything as much as possible."

"But" Ian replies, "What do you do when you don't feel good and are sad, or angry, or hurting in some way?"

Bry blinks his brilliant red eyes and says "Good! You are listening closely to what I am saying, and this is very good for both of us. When you are not feeling good, your immediate goal is to find something that will make you feel just a little better than you were when you were feeling sad. This can be something as simple as taking a walk outside in the fresh air or looking at vistas that are far away. You can reread a book that you already like or start one that you have not yet read. Listen to some good music, the classical type that your father listens to. If you ask him, he will say it is baroque music which, is uplifting and helps the mind and brain relax in a certain way. You can go and practice your favorite sport. It is very difficult to go from sad to happy in one step. The best way is to inch up the emotional ladder one step at a time. As you train your mind to do small steps, your feelings will improve faster and faster."

"Do you have an understanding of this now?"

Ian nods his head up and down and says, "Yes."

"Good" Bry replies, "You see, Ian, when you are feeling good, your mind and body are vibrating at a higher frequency level than when you are not feeling good. This may sound a little simple but it is really the starting point for making your dreams come true. It is the basis of learning and how to develop creative thinking and goal setting."

Ian has a troubled look in his eyes so Bry stops and waits for the question that he knows is coming. "Bry, I don't know what you mean by vibration and frequency."

Chapter Three
Everything Is Moving

FREQUENCY AND VIBRATION are words that describe energy. Everything in the world and in the cosmos is in constant motion. Energy is what forms matter into the things that you see and touch. Matter is molded into different things when the frequency of the energy is changed. Vibration is just the description of how the energy is moving. Do you recall what the waves looks like when you throw a stone into a pool of water? Can you see in your mind the motion of the ripples in the water which come out from a center where the rock hits the water?"

Ian takes a moment to remember the fun of throwing pebbles and stones into the lake. He sees the splash and the small circle of waves that go across the still water. He looks at Bry and says, "Yes I remember what that looks and feels like. It's a lot of fun skipping rocks on the water. How does that represent vibration and frequency?"

"Ah, that is a very good question my young apprentice," Bry responds. "Let me explain it this way. Think of the little waves that flow across the top of the water as representing the movement or motion of energy in the form of a vibration. The space between the top of each wave represents frequency. The larger the space is the lower the frequency. The shorter the distance, the higher the frequency. All of this is just energy that is moving. Even the most solid item is really a mass of motion, vibration, and frequency and therefore, energy. Do you have a better understanding of the concept now?"

Ian looks at Bry for moment and Bry sees that Ian is thinking deeply over the information that he has just received. Bry is pleased to watch his new student thinking so seriously. He knows that for Ian to learn he must understand a concept to the fullest of his ability. As Ian learns, he will grow in knowledge and be able to grasp greater and greater insights.

Ian looks at Bry and tilts his head a little to the side and replies, "Bry, I still have a problem with something that appears solid, like a rock or piece of wood, or my pocketknife not being solid. All of these items seem very hard and strong so how can they be energy?"

Bry smiles his loving smile at Ian and thinks to himself, what a wonderful question for Ian to ask. He then responds, "All of the items you spoke of appear to be different, yet they are all the same at the smallest level. Let me explain. Do you remember reading about the ancient Greek civilization in your history books at school?"

Ian nods, "Yes."

"The Greeks understood that everything physical was made up of the same thing. They called these "things" atoms, and said they were the smallest part of everything in the whole world. So their logic dictated that in order for there to be different material objects, the atoms had to be arranged in different combinations. How the atoms are arranged is done by using different vibrations and frequencies. The ancient Greeks did not have an understanding of vibration and frequency, but they did know that some sort of energy or force was responsible for objects being different from one another. Let's look at another example of frequency. After the rain storm of last week, do you remember seeing a rainbow in the late afternoon sky?"

Ian shakes his head "Yes" but wonders

how Bry knew about the storm.

"Good," Bry replies and he continues. "The colors of the rainbow are individual vibrations or frequencies that are part of natural sunlight. When the sunlight strikes water drops in the air at just the right angle the water will cause the different colors to become visible. Each color is a different frequency and the sunlight is light energy which is in motion. All of the colors together appear as normal light but each frequency is very distinct. By mixing the colors in different amounts all kinds of new colors can be created and each new creation is a different frequency but they are all still energy that is moving.

It was a lot of fun and work helping the Greeks acquire their knowledge of science, mathematics, geometry, and medicine. We dragons have been helping mankind for a very long time."

Ian is looking at Bry and his eyes get big from hearing that dragons have been influencing people. He asks, "Please tell me more about dragons and what they do."

Bry stretches a little and smiles at Ian. He then says, "Why yes, of course Ian, but to return to the topic at hand, do you have a better understanding on the basic concept of energy?"

Ian looks at Bry and rubs his fingers under his chin and reflects about this new knowledge. "I think I have an idea of what you are saying but I will need more time. It is difficult to grasp something that can't be seen."

Chapter Four
The Power of the Clan

PERHAPS THIS IS A GOOD TIME to take a small break from our lesson and listen to a good dragon story. I have not told you very much about my dragon friends or about my clan. So please, relax on the grass with your back against the stone wall, and I will tell you some history."

Ian moves over to the edge of the stone wall and sits with his back against the warm stones. The coolness of the green grass is comforting as he crosses his legs and listens.

"Remember when we first met I showed you some of the world's past and that dragons were part of that past?" Ian nods yes. "Well, dragons were on the earth before the dinosaurs. We were created by the Great Creator for this planet as the first beings with the capability to become thinkers of who and what we are. We were designed with brains that would allow us to learn and to become wise if we chose to do so. It is the same option that is given to mankind from the Creator. We both have the same basic make up.

Over much time, as in millions of years, dragons did choose to learn and become wise. It was not an easy choice to make. We made many of the same mistakes that people do, but from those mistakes we learned to correct them and to make better choices. At one time, dragons did fight with each other and have wars. We acted out of anger and not love. We believed in the power of the group and not the individual. We caused each other, and ourselves, much pain and suffering. We learned our lessons the hard way, just as

humans are doing now. In every period of time, there were always a few dragons that understood what the correct way to live is. They slowly taught other dragons their philosophies. Eventually, we became peaceful with each other and with the world around us. We devoted ourselves to knowledge.

In the dragon books that your mother found for you there are descriptions of how dragons live and what their lineage or clans are composed of. A lot of the information in the books is correct because we helped the authors write them, even if they did not have direct contact with a dragon. We can influence a creative person with our thoughts, but always in a positive and loving way.

My name, for example, Bry-Ankh, has a very special meaning. "Bry" is my individual name, but "Ankh" is the name of my clan or family. There have been many "Ankhs" throughout our history. When you read your books on ancient Egypt did you notice a certain symbol that the Egyptians used?"

Ian reflected for a moment and then he did remember that the Egyptians had a symbol that was called the ANKH.

"Yes, Bry, I do remember a symbol that sounds just like your name, and I think the ancient Egyptians called it "the key of life." Does it have a meaning for you? Is there a mystery about it because I love a good mystery?"

Bry nods his head and replies, "Yes, there are many mysteries from that time in history. You are correct in your memory as the Egyptian ankh is indeed the key of life and much more. Let me show you how important it is to my clan." Ian looks at Bry and notices a golden glow start to form on his chest. The glow intensifies and becomes a living flame that takes the shape of a circle that is resting on top of two lines that form a

T. It moves and dances like a fire of brilliant gold. Ian is thrilled and excited to observe this phenomenon as it is most unusual.

Ian watches the shape and sees Bry close his eyes and concentrate. The shape moves away from Bry's body and stands in front of him. Ian can feel the intense energy that is emanating from the symbol, yet the dancing flames give off no heat. Ian feels an immense feeling of love come over him and is almost teary eyed from the energy. It is then that the symbol changes to a brilliant golden-white color and then disappears with a flash of light.

Ian blinks and Bry opens his eyes and lets out a slow, long breath. He looks at Ian and smiles and Ian impulsively reaches out and gives Bry a big hug, Bry instinctively curls his tail around Ian's feet. Both of them are a little surprised by this action but each of them laughs at this gesture at the same time.

Chapter Five
The Ankh

IAN REALIZES THAT THE HAIR on his head is sticking out a little, like it does when a balloon is rubbed and creates static electricity. He is tingly all over and has a warm feeling in his heart. Bry smiles and says, "The feelings you are having are from the intense love energy that is contained in the symbol of the ankh. The symbol, which is a key, was given to the ancient Egyptians from my clan. We had perfected its life force and power long before the Pharaohs used it."

Ian is excited about the idea of dragons helping the Egyptians and wants to learn more of what they did and how they helped the Pharaohs of the ancient world. "Bry, did you help the Pharaohs and wisemen of Egypt?" Bry shakes his head with a "no" motion and says, "My cousin, Ra-Ankh, was the mentor to that civilization. They honored him by using his first name, Ra, as their reference to the sun god. To them, he appeared as a glowing ball of light, so it was easy to make the connection. They were very eager to learn and at first used the knowledge for good and noble purposes. Their culture was structured to honor the living and the dead. They developed great spiritual rites and rituals around the dying process. The priesthood was a very powerful order. Ra explained the power of the ankh and what it represented."

"What is the power of the ankh?" Ian asked with a quizzical look on his face.

The idea of the symbol being something magical and powerful has Ian thinking in

many directions. What can it do? What does it mean? Can it be used now? Is it a weapon or a doorway to something greater? Bry sees the mind of Ian turning and questioning so he starts to explain before Ian can ask questions.

"Ian, the ankh has great power, and it represents the door to different dimensions of time and space. It is one of the keys to life and death, but there is no real dying, just a change of energy and vibration. The symbol contains two separate shapes. The first is the T which forms the base upon which the top portion sits, which is an ellipse. The base represents the three dimensions of height, width, and depth. This is the physical world of the three dimensions upon which everything in the cosmos is built. It gives you the reference of time and distance so that there are points of measurement. Any questions so far?"

Ian shakes his head with a vigorous "yes" motion but tells Bry to just continue with his story. "A point of measurement also defines to you what "time" means and the way you measure and keep track of it. Time is a part of the physical world.

The top part of the symbol is an ellipse. That is the geometric figure that has two focal points or radiuses. Do you remember this from your geometry class at school?" Again Ian nods a yes. "Now, the two centers are joined together by an outer line which forms the ellipse, and this represents the two worlds of life and death, that is, the birth and rebirth of everything in the universe. Because the centers are bound by the outer line, it also means that nothing is ever lost. Now, what is most amazing is that when the physical properties of the base are energized and focused through the top, a doorway to the cosmos is opened and time and space become one. It is by using this energy that dragons can manipulate time. Remember that I told you in our first meeting that dragons can do this and that no one will notice that you and I have been engaged in being with each other?"

Ian does indeed remember and the idea of learning this is very exciting. He asks Bry, "Is this something that I can do? Can I be as powerful as a dragon and be like you?"

Bry looks at Ian and smiles that all too familiar loving smile and replies, "All things are possible when you have the correct knowledge. However, this is something that you will most likely not acquire in this lifetime. Perhaps in one of many more that will come."

Ian thinks about what he means by "*many more that will come*" but before he can ask a question, Bry continues with his story. "If you will notice, many of the pictures or hieroglyphics that are on the ancient Egyptians ruins show the Pharaoh holding the ankh by the ellipse. He is doing this to show the energy doorway between the worlds of physical and spiritual dimensions. He is allowing the energy from below the base of the symbol to travel through the symbol and then to him so that he can access a higher level of existence."

"But why does the Pharaoh want to get to a different place?" Ian asks. "And what is a higher level of existence?"

"A wonderful question, Ian." Bry answers, "The Pharaoh, when he was protecting his people, wanted to get information to help with food production, weather conditions, or the movements of his enemies. When unanswered questions about running the country in a prosperous and safe manner could not be found, the Pharaoh used the power of the ankh to find the answer. Each succeeding Pharaoh used the ankh correctly and for hundreds of years my cousin assisted them. But slowly, Pharaohs of the future started to use the power for personal riches and glory, and to enslave their own people. It was then that Ra refused to help them. In the past, Ra always kept key components of the ankh secret and would only show a Pharaoh how to use the power when he was sure of the Pharaoh's good intentions.

You also asked about *higher levels* and what they are. A higher level is a place where the energy is moving faster than it is here on Earth. In such a place, all known knowledge may be kept or any of the Creator's creations may exist. They are places where the laws of time and space do not apply. There are places where the non-physical part of you and I exist, which is eternal. There is much more to this wondrous universe of creation than men, and even dragons, are aware of. The ankh is protected and used by my clan. We honor what it can do and we are grateful that the Creator allowed us to find its power and purpose."

Chapter Six
Bry Has Friends

IAN'S MIND IS GOING IN A HUNDRED different directions. He is excited by the idea of dragons influencing history and wants to know more. Does Bry have other family? Are there other dragons here, right now, which are helping people or watching events? Will he get to see and talk with any of Bry's friends? Does Bry have any children or hatchlings? What are dragons seeking or doing for new knowledge? How much *more* is there to learn?

Bry leans back on his rear legs and chuckles a bit to himself as he watches Ian's mind. He is impressed with all of the wonder and questions that Ian has but is reluctant to tell him that he can also listen in on what he is thinking and feeling. Bry is thrilled that Ian is his student and is sure that Ian will gain confidence and wisdom as he grows older. A mind that is curious and teachable does not come along very often. The world can be changed by just one person and Bry wonders if Ian will be that person.

Bry collects his composure and looks Ian in the eye, takes a nice long breath, and says, "Ian you have so much going on in your head and in your heart right now. Just take a few minutes to relax and feel the warmth of the day. Look at the bright blue sky and the puffy clouds. Smell the intoxicating aroma from the flowers in your mother's delightful courtyard. Be present here and now, and know that all of your questions will be answered. Remember, this is a universe of receiving what you ask for, whenever you are really ready to hear

the answers. It is a law in this universe and it must be obeyed."

Ian blinks a few times and realizes that his thoughts are running out of control and that his emotions are heightened. He now senses that his heart is racing and he is breathing faster than normal, with a little bit of perspiration on his forehead. He looks at Bry and sees that all-calming smile and then everything slows down. He starts to sit back down but instead runs over to Bry and once again gives him a giant hug. This time neither of them is surprised and Bry places the bottom of his jaw around Ian's shoulder and gives him a gentle squeeze of his own. Both of them are now relaxed and now Ian does sit down and crosses his legs.

Bry takes a few moments to study his pupil's body language and to listen to his thinking. Then he resumes his story. "Ian, you wanted to know if I have any family of my own or other dragon friends. I do have both, but for right now I will just tell you about a very dear and wonderful friend of mine from the Far East, what you know as China.

Thousands of years ago while I was a slightly younger dragon, I was studying Chinese art and medicine when I met a very beautiful and wise dragon by the name of Shar-Ming. She is an extraordinarily beautiful dragon. Her scales are brilliant green with wisps of golden thread that appear to be in a random order. Her eyes are as bright as diamonds in the sun. When she moves, it looks like sparkling, living green water. She is truly a magnificent water dragon. We became very dear friends and spent a lot of time together talking art, philosophy, and the future possibilities of man's civilizations. She taught me about the ancient Chinese energy system called the *I Ching*. She was the dragon who brought it to the Chinese. She did this before the great Chinese philosopher Confucius was her student. His accomplishments were a great sense of pride for Shar-Ming. Confucius used the system in his teachings. Later on, she was the advisor to the Chinese emperor who used her last name to start the Ming Dynasties. Her name in Chinese would have been Ming-Shar as the Chinese use the last name first. Her dragon name is Shar-Ming as Ming is her clan name. The Ming clans are all water dragons and prefer to live in the Far East around beautiful oceans and lakes. She was much honored to be named a part of Chinese culture. If she is willing, I will ask her if she would like to come and visit you someday. She is fiercely loyal to her friends and will help you as much as she can. If she comes, you must be appreciative of her efforts and try your best. Shar-Ming is a very good teacher."

The idea of other dragons teaching people is fascinating to Ian. He wants to see and learn from any dragon that will appear to him. And a special friend of Bry's is just that much more exciting. Ian asks, "Do you think she will come for a visit? I would love to hear what she has to say. I read about Chinese culture and society. They had a very advanced civilization according to my history books. And what about Ra, could I meet him too? This is just so wonderful that you have friends and family."

Bry is amused by the passion of his young student. It has been a long time since he has had an opportunity to work with anyone of Ian's ability. Of course, Ian does not know of his potential, but Bry sees the future in ways that can only be described as incredible. He sees the images in Ian's mind as tiny puzzle pieces that are illuminated by small, bright flashes of light. It is like watching little cameras take pictures and freezing them in space. Bry knows that just one man at just the right moment can change everything. He hopes Ian will be that man. But that is a future that only Ian can create and only if Ian applies himself and studies will he be able to do anything.

Bry is still sitting in front of Ian with a wisp of a grin on his face and a tail that is swishing slightly back and forth. This aspect is a source of great pleasure for both of the cats which have not left. They perceive the tail as large silver play toy. They are taking turns pouncing at Bry's tail. This act is amusing to Bry and he lets them continue with their play.

Bry replies to Ian and says, "Young one, you have a lot of questions and it is nice that you find my stories enjoyable. We dragons love telling good stories, especially to someone who has a keen interest in learning from them. You wanted to know about meeting Shar-Ming and my cousin Ra. Well, I will get a message to Shar-Ming. I have not seen her for a long time and I do miss conversation with her. Besides that, she has the most delightful fragrance of jasmine about her which is just intoxicating. Dragons are very fond of fragrances. As to Ra, that will be a bit harder. He is not on this planet any longer. He used the power of the ankh to open a portal, or something your scientists might call a "stargate," and went on a journey to visit a few other earthlike star systems. He likes to travel and see other life forms that the Creator has made. The Creator has a great sense of humor and there is so much more life out in this big universe of which man has absolutely no knowledge.

I can, however, if you are interested, take you on a trip in time back to ancient Egypt and observe Ra. You see, what has already happened is recorded, and I can access that information and view it much the same way that you might see a big screen movie or a video."

Chapter Seven
A Trip Back in Time

IAN IS EXTREMELY EXCITED about this possibility and jumps up from his sitting position and says, "Absolutely! I want to take a trip!"

"Excellent," Bry says, "I will touch the top of your head much the same way that I did when we first met but this time I will go with you to help explain what you are seeing, hearing and feeling."

With that being said, Bry reaches out and taps Ian on the top of his head. Everything spins in a kaleidoscope of colored light, and just as quickly it all stops and they are both standing in front of a structure that Ian has only seen in history books.

"Welcome to the Egypt that was," Bry says and turns to face his young traveler. Ian then notices that Bry is not Bry but looks just like an Egyptian. How wonderful is this! Then the new Bry speaks, "You see me as what would be called a scribe in the ancient world. My job is to record what the Pharaoh, or some other person of authority, would say. I am a records-keeper for the royal family. You and I can see each other but just like back home, no one else can. We are just observers but we can experience everything just like it happened the first time for the people who are here. We are standing in front of the great temple of Karnak that is alongside the beautiful Nile River. This is a place of religious and cultural expression. Let us walk into the temple and see the beauty of this magical place."

They proceed to enter the great temple and Ian notices the thirty-plus-foot high

stone columns that are adorned with colorful artwork depicting life for the Egyptians. On top of the columns are huge stone blocks that make up the ceiling, and they too, just like the columns, are covered with color and pictures. The inside is much cooler than in the hot sun and a mild breeze works its way around and through the structure. The air carries the pleasing scent of an unknown fragrance, but it is delightful to smell. Spaced evenly about the temple are golden and bronze stands that contain some sort of liquid that is burning. These give off enough light to easily see all of the pictures. Hanging between some of the columns are large sheets of fine fabric which gently move back and forth in the gentle wind. In the distance, Ian hears music that is mild and soothing but the notes are from instruments that he is not familiar with. The first impression is both awe inspiring and comforting, but combined into the same feeling, an interesting blend of sensations.

Bry is walking alongside his student and watching what is being viewed by Ian. Bry is happy to notice the keen interest and the questions that are popping up. He stops for a moment and says, "Let me start to explain some of what you are seeing. The pictures on all the stone work are what you call *hieroglyphics*. These are a form of picture-language that the average Egyptian can understand. Most of the population cannot read or write but they can understand what the pictures represent. The only people who use just letters for writing are the priests, scribes, and the members of the royal families. Formal education is reserved for only the most privileged of this society. It is easier to govern a nation when just a few have access to all the knowledge.

The burning stands that supply the inside light are using oil that is called saffron. It burns very brightly, yet gives little or no smoke while burning. This way there is no residue which will hide any of the artwork and pictures. There are small bowls that are placed throughout the temple which contain a substance that is called incense. The incense will burn slowly and gives off the wonderful fragrance that you smell. It also produces an odor that insects don't like. This helps to keep the area free of mosquitoes and pesky flies. The large sheets between some of the columns are made from either silk or very fine cotton that grows along the banks of the Nile River. The river is a highway which carries all of the riches and necessities for daily use throughout all of Egypt. To many, the river is a sacred entity and is viewed as the giver of life.

The music that you hear in the background is from instruments made of wood, stone, and metal. They do not have anything like brass horns that you might see in a marching band or in an orchestra. Those have not yet been invented but what they do have will make beautiful music."

They keep walking deeper into the temple complex and Ian sees what appear to be servants carrying many different gold and silver plates full of food, fruit, berries, and vessels that he believes hold some kind of liquid. He watches the servants doing their duties and both he and Bry follow along behind to see where the plates are going. Both of them are looking at the beautiful art and the fine fabrics when they turn a corner and there before them is a huge throne room. It is magnificent, with a golden throne sitting at the top of a small flight of stairs. On each side of the golden chair are statues of Egyptian gods that are adorned with gold and silver bracelets, neck chains, and head coverings. They are almost as tall as the columns holding up the massive ceiling. Several incense bowls are giving off a wonderful fragrance while tables are placed around the room with all of the food and drink. Ian notices finely dressed men and beautiful women in discussions, eating and laughing as they enjoy the dancers that are performing.

Chapter Eight
A Pharaoh's Entrance

ALL OF A SUDDEN, four very large warriors enter the chamber. Each is holding a heavy metal disk and carrying a long baton. They stop at the bottom of the stairs and simultaneously strike the disks and with loud voices cry, "All will now be still and bow thee down and behold the living god, Pharaoh of all Egypt, the great and all powerful Om-Seti, ruler of all that he sees!"

Ian is wide eyed and amazed from what he is seeing and hearing. He looks over at Bry who is smiling. Bry quickly tells him that he is translating the Egyptian words into English so that he can understand what is being said.

Ian is impressed by the mighty warriors, with their gleaming swords and body armor. The authority in their commands is followed by instant compliance from the other members of the assembly. As they bow, a drummer enters the room beating a large drum with a steady rhythm of walking. He is followed by two standard bearers. One has a golden staff with a curved top and a crossbar in the middle of it. The other has the same symbol that Bry had showed Ian earlier, who now knows that this is the symbol for the powerful and mystical ankh. It too is made of gold but it seems to have a small but noticeable radiant light surrounding it. The standard bearers take up positions on each side of the great throne.

The drummer marches to the front of the throne at the bottom of the steps, then stops beating his drum. Silence is in the room and then the great Pharaoh, Om-Seti, enters.

The very air in the room seems to change and become electric as Om-Seti enters and proceeds to take his position upon the great throne.

Om-Seti is a powerful looking man with a muscular and toned body. Dark eyes look out from his slightly oval face with a gaze of complete control over all that he sees. The breastplate of gold and silver that graces his chest has many precious gemstones. On his head is the two-pointed hat that represents the Upper and Lower Kingdoms of the Nile River. Around the band of this hat is a flat, gold chain and the two points are covered with silver tips. His shirt or tunic is of fine, white silk with a belt of golden thread around his waist. Shoes, or better said, tall sandals, are secured about his feet with straps of leather that have inlaid gold and come halfway up his lower leg. His complexion is slightly almond in color, which is somewhere between the olive of the northern Mediterranean people and the natives of Africa. He is the Pharaoh, ruler of all the land of Egypt and feared by his enemies throughout the ancient world. He has not yet said a single word, yet his presence is pure power and control.

Ian notices another person enter the room who looks just like Bry. He is holding a large scroll and is trailed by servants who have writing tools and more scrolls. Bry leans over to Ian and says, "That person is the royal scribe. It is his job to record all of the important items of today's discussions. Any rule or command given by the great Om-Seti will be written down as any decision he may make will become instant law. It is important that commands be followed completely and that they can be carried throughout the land by other scribes and given to the people."

Ian looks at Bry and asks, "That scribe looks just like you. Is it or was it you? Were you the scribe to Om-Seti? Were you in Egypt with your cousin Ra?"

"No, that is not me, I thought it would be fun for you to see me as a royal scribe. I was one to a Pharaoh but that happened much later, long after Ra had left and stopped helping. But for now, let's go for a walk. What is about to happen next is the day to day business of ruling the land. People will approach the great Om-Seti to ask for a favor or a ruling over a dispute. He will listen to each request then make a decision, then the scribe will make a record that will be obeyed. He will be finished in a few hours. Then we can come back and observe Om-Seti and Ra as they talk with each other."

The idea of seeing Ra, Bry's powerful cousin, is an exciting opportunity. Both Bry and Ian leave the great temple and walk towards the gleaming Nile River. On the river are small sailboats and large barrages.

The barges are being moved either by ox from the shore with long ropes or by men rowing with large oars. Ian can see that the men rowing are slaves or perhaps captured warriors from a conquered country. A large man with a whip in his hand stands above the slaves, giving orders and occasionally cracking his whip above their heads. Ian is quick to see the differences between those who have privilege and those who do not. It is a world of great contrast as there is little cooperation, only competition and control. There are most definitely the "haves and have nots" in this culture.

Bry explains to Ian that in this world there is little in the way of mechanical devices of which he is familiar. Most jobs are accomplished with manpower and the help of animals such as oxen, horses, donkeys, or elephants. Manpower is the most plentiful labor force, and the use of slaves is common and part of the culture. Just because it is part of the culture does not make it right, but it is still the custom of the day. Being a free man is a luxury, and if you and your family are free, then you are indeed in a lucky group.

Both Bry and Ian sit under the shade of a tall palm tree and watch the river traffic and the fishermen casting their nets and then beating the water with wooden paddles to scare the fish into the nets. It seems to be a simple way of life for some and not so simple for others, but there is a sense of order as the day unfolds. Time is only measured by the movement of the sun, and Ian can see it is getting closer to setting in the western horizon and he wonders if it is time to observe the Pharaoh and Ra. Bry is also aware that it is time to go back to the temple but they linger a little longer by the river. Bry has such fond memories of his time spent in Egypt. He has a great compassion for the people of this land and the ancient wisdom and teachings that were part of this wonderful, and at times enlightened, civilization. He takes one final breath of the fragrances from the day and then waves to Ian, and they both start back to the temple.

Chapter Nine
Ra Revealed

THEY RETRACE THEIR PATH and enter the temple. Ian follows Bry as they walk the now quiet corridors of this mystical place. The throne room that was just a short time ago full of people and energy is now softly lit by the few torches which are still burning. Bry goes to a part of the room that has a large decorative linen hanging from the ceiling which is supported by chains of silver. He pulls back one side to reveal an opening in the wall which is large enough to walk through. Ian sees that the dark corridor has a soft glow coming from the far end. They slowly walk towards the light which is getting brighter as they near the end of the pathway and the entrance to another chamber. They quietly walk into the light and there before them is a truly magnificent sight.

This chamber is not as large as the main throne room but in the middle of it is a huge black granite throne with flat, gold-inlaid chains and sparkling jewels which appear to be large diamonds. On each side are golden torch stands burning with saffron oil and another fragrance which smells like red roses. The same odor as the one that Ian's mother has in her flower garden in the courtyard back home. In front of the throne is a large glowing crystal that has a place hollowed out on the top of it. Ian can see that the crystal is holding the mystical and powerful ankh which is now glowing much brighter than before. In front of the ankh, facing the throne, is the great Om-Seti, who is sitting on a small golden bench seat and looking towards the

throne. However, the most impressive sight in the room is what is occupying the middle of the throne. There on the other side of the ankh, facing Om-Seti, is what can only be called a miniature sun. It is a ball of brightly glowing light and fire that seems to have a life energy of its own. It is not sitting on the throne but is hovering a few inches above the seat. There is a small crackle in the air and a feeling of static electricity.

Ian looks to Bry and Bry nods his head, "Yes," and Ian knows that he is in the presence of Ra, Bry's cousin. There is a sense of great love in the room, and even though there is power, mystery, and wisdom, a presence of calmness and control is also noticeable. Om-Seti is in deep concentration and Ian can tell he wants to ask Ra some questions for guidance. As they are observing, Ian hears the great Pharaoh talk to Ra.

"Oh great, wise, and powerful Ra, I am in need of answers. My priests are insisting that the people and I embrace and worship more gods of the earth, sky, and water. I believe, as my predecessor the great Pharaoh Akhenaten did, that there is only one source for all of creation. I have heard of the rumors that he was murdered for his beliefs by his own priests. I do not want this to happen to me but I also want to take power away from these greedy and manipulative members of our religion. Oh great Ra, what should I do?"

The force upon the granite throne vibrates and the light intensifies. A strong and confident voice is then heard throughout the chamber. "Om-Seti, you are wise and correct to seek my advice on this matter. You are right in your beliefs. There is only one creative force in this entire universe. The all-powerful, I AM THAT I AM, he who is eternal and ever to all-everlasting, the one and only Creator. You should be wary of your priests, as they work for themselves, not for you or your people. They have learned how to trick your people into believing that they, and only they, can bring someone safely into the next life. They are consumed with the need for more power. They hide the truth from everyone that what the Creator has freely given to you, you can never lose. A belief that is left unchallenged is dangerous. People who lack knowledge are easily swayed by wicked tongues.

Akhenaten was indeed assassinated by his own priests. You must guard your family and your rule from these parasites. You should tell your priests that you are more of a god than any other that they may conjure up. This will make them unhappy but it will not fill them with rage. That would happen if you insisted upon them worshiping only one true God. Secretly pass on your belief to your family and successors. It will be a long time before your way of thinking is accepted, but eventually it will be. Would you like to have a conversation with Akhenaten and let him tell you with his own words how he can help you in your present circumstance?"

Chapter Ten
Akhenaten Speaks

Y ES, GREAT ONE, I think that would be very helpful at this moment. His perspective would be greatly appreciated."

"Om-Seti, place your hand upon the ankh and push it firmly into the crystal base. It will then energize and open a gate to the next dimension and there, I will summon Akhenaten."

Om-Seti does as he is instructed and the crystal base glows with an intense white light which travels up the device, through his hand, and out into the chamber. Four brilliant beams of light strike large diamonds which are evenly spaced on tall columns in the room. The beams are then redirected and hit a central point above the back of the great, dark throne. A portal of light starts to grow and enlarge until it reaches the ceiling of the room. Within the opening, a figure of a man starts to form and Ian can see that it is another Pharaoh as he is dressed in a very similar way to Om-Seti. The figure becomes more solid but still seems to be glowing with some kind of internal energy of its own.

Bry leans closer to Ian and whispers in his ear, "You are seeing Akhenaten the same way Om-Seti saw him. Life goes into life, which goes into more life. It is the eternal gift from the Great Creator. Nothing is ever wasted. Now listen to their dialog. It will be important to you later on."

Om-Seti takes his hand off of the ankh and sits down on the small, golden bench. Om-Seti hesitates for a few seconds to collect his thoughts. He is aware that he is being

given a rare and magnificent gift from Ra and Akhenaten. Akhenaten fixes his eyes upon the present Pharaoh and starts to speak. "Great Om-Seti, I am pleased that you have asked for my insight to your political issues. It is true that I was killed by my own priests. I made the mistake of insisting that my people and my priests all worship the single god, the Great Creator. I knew it to be true that the Great Creator is responsible for all that is. I moved too quickly with my beliefs. My people were not ready for this. They were not ready for the ideas of personal responsibility and the fundamentals of physical creating. They needed real representations to understand the world they lived in and my priests were all too willing to give them what they asked for. It was a cunning and devious way for the priests to gain unearned value and riches from my people.

You can avoid my fate and protect your ideas and your family, but you must do as I say. You need to start a secret society. It will be called the Brotherhood of the One. Ra and I will send candidates to you that believe as you do. You and they will meet in secret or in disguise. You will be taught by Ra and me the truths of creation. The steps for success will be given to you as well as the laws of this universe. We will help you to learn them and preserve them. This Brotherhood will in time keep all of mankind from the darkness of ignorance and hate. This is your decision to make. I cannot make it for you but if you decide to follow this path, it will be more rewarding than you can possibly imagine. What say you, O great Om-Seti?"

Om-Seti is silent for a moment and Ian can see that he is carefully considering Akhenaten's offer. Om-Seti gets up from his bench, looks into the eyes of the former

Pharaoh, bows his head in a form of respect, and answers with just one word, "Yes."

"Wonderful," Akhenaten replies, and with a clap of his hands and a short bow from his head, he is gone and the light goes out of the room as the portal closes.

Ian can hear Ra say to Om-Seti, "You have chosen wisely. You will be given instructions in dreams or in this room. You will start a light in the hearts and minds of select men and women which will survive when all else seems to be gone. No one will know but those who have decided to take this journey with you and the ones who come after them. The Great Creator knows of your decision and is pleased. This I can tell you because the Creator wants to honor your choice: All is well with you, great Om-Seti."

Ian and Bry see the glow of Ra diminish and they know that the conversation is over.

The ankh as well as the crystal base return to their normal state and silence is in the great throne room. Om-Seti turns and walks back up the corridor that leads to his normal life but he now knows that this life will never be the same. He has a radiant smile upon his face and a feeling of great love in his heart. Om-Seti is at peace with what he is about to do.

Ian takes a moment to look at Bry then gives him a huge bear hug of appreciation for what he has seen and heard. Ian turns to look once more upon the great Ra to say a quick goodbye. As he is doing this, he notices that the miniature sun is changing shape and starting to look like a dragon. Not just any dragon but a Silver Dragon and it smiles at Ian the same way that Bry does. Then it winks at him!

Ian looks back to Bry who is grinning broadly at Ian and simply says, "Ian there is a lot to learn about dragons." Bry then reaches out and touches Ian on the top of his head. Ian sees a bright flash of light and they are once again home in Ian's mother's courtyard.

Chapter Eleven
The First Lesson

BEFORE IAN CAN ASK ANY MORE QUESTIONS, he sees his mother coming. She looks over towards the swimming pool and asks the revelers to be careful and not let their music get too loud. She also reminds them to be mindful of the horseplay as it would not be a good idea to make an emergency trip to the hospital. With that being said, she heads out towards where Ian, Bry, and the two cats are sitting. Ian gives Bry a worried look because he is afraid of being seen with his new dragon friend. Bry gives Ian that all too familiar smile and says, "Don't be worried my young student, your mother cannot tell that we are here. I have raised the vibration level of our conversation and we are virtually invisible to her. She may, however, notice a fragrance that is about. I enjoy adding a little texture to the air as it gives it a life of its own."

Just as Bry has finished his comment, Ian notices that his mother is sniffing the air as though she is looking for the source of some unknown but pleasing aroma. She looks around at the plants and flowers, smiles, but Ian can see that she has no idea where the pleasant scent is coming from.

Bry waves to his student and says, "Let's go for a walk to the lake. We can discuss our time travel while we walk. I used this method of teaching with the ancient Greeks. Nature can provide a variety of visuals." They start out for the lake, all four of them, cats included. For the cats, this is a great adventure for along with the continuing interest in a bright silvery, play toy, they may encounter other

foes that will need to be vanquished.

As they cross the bright green pasture towards the lake, Bry starts to talk about their Egyptian trip. "Ian, Om-Seti and the Brotherhood of the One were given four parts to the learning process and they are as follows:

- The first part is who do you allow to teach you, that is, who do you listen to.
- Next, there is the idea of being teachable, which has two sides to it. One is the willingness to learn something and the other is whether you are willing to change something once you have learned a new or different idea or task.
- The life balance scale is our third point and it too has two parts to it. The first half of the scale is where all the thinking takes place and other half of the scale is the action, or doing, side. The important part is to learn to know that each side is not equal in the

amount of effort which is required in order to achieve proper balance. The thinking side of the scale should take up most of your time at first. Even as much as ninety percent of what you want to do. Thinking is a vital part of goal achievement. But it is important to understand that once your thinking has given you a clear vision of what is to be done, you must shift to the action side of the scale. You cannot just stay on the thinking side and put little or no effort into your desires. Dreams are achieved with hard, consistent work, but it will be fun to do.

- The last step in learning has four sections in it and they are a little more complicated to understand. Step one is being aware of *not knowing* that you don't know. Step two is *knowing that you don't know.* Step three is *knowing something and that you have to work at it to make it happen.* And step four is *knowing something and having the results happen automatically without having to think about making something happen.*

These four basic steps are the four cornerstones of all of learning. It is your goal to learn these four basic steps. In time you should try to become a master of each one. This will be a lifetime commitment but a fun one, I promise.

Ian blinks his eyes and takes a long, slow breath. In his look, Bry can see that Ian is confused. He lets him take his time to ponder what he has been told. Ian looks at Bry and asks, "Bry, I have an idea of what you are saying but the whole process seems complicated and difficult. How can anyone learn something if the rules for learning are what you say they are? This is a most difficult task."

Bry replies, "Ian, remember our Egyptian experience. The same knowledge that I am giving you was given to Om-Seti and to the Brotherhood of the One. It has not changed because it is the truth. The road to knowledge is both long and complicated at times. It is a journey, but it should be fun to take. It will take dedication and time to become a master at something. I will say this many times to you. A concept may take five minutes to learn but a lifetime to master. But once the basic steps are learned, they can be used to master anything that you wish to accomplish. There is no limit to what you can do once you have the proper foundation."

Chapter Twelve
The Path of a Master

THIS MAKES IAN FEEL a little better and makes the task of learning seem a little less challenging. Besides, Ian likes the idea of becoming a master of something. The problem is Ian has no idea of what he is wanting to master. Ian says to Bry "I am interested in being a master but I have no idea of what I want to do. Where do I start and how do I get somewhere?" With this statement, Ian walks in a small circle and waves his arms in the air in an expression of frustration.

Bry stands still and looks at young Ian with a small and gratifying grin of his own. He is very pleased with Ian's reaction because it tells Bry that Ian is taking this seriously and that it means something to him. Ian is a good student and Bry is glad and happy to be his teacher.

When Ian has calmed down and Bry knows that he is once again ready to learn, he says, "Young one, it is good to see your frustration but do not be disheartened about the process. You have plenty of time to accomplish goals and desires. Try to be happy now and look for something good in which you can believe. Your path to knowledge will grow in direct proportion to your ability to feel good. Your mind can only hold so much new information before it becomes full. Then you must stop and rest. Take a moment to contemplate what you have been told and seen today. Let the lessons become a part of you. Becoming a master is accomplished both with the mind and the body. As the mind gets more information, it will change the vibration of

your body and therefore your body will help your mind to grow. It is a cycle in which one will help the other. The objective is to raise your entire vibration so that you reach the last state of learning, which is to know and have automatic mastery.

Now, let's go back and review the first of the four parts of learning. This is our lesson for today. We will start with the first concept of who do you listen to. Do you remember that we talked about this earlier today? We will discuss the issues of feeling, observing, and your emotions in greater detail. This will be the only item that we work on. Are you ready for a new adventure? Do you want to expand your abilities?"

Ian stops moving for a moment, takes a long, slow breath and looks Bry in the eye and only says one word, "Yes."

"Wonderful," Bry responds. "Who you listen to is a vital step forward. Information you choose to receive must be useful and believable. You should pay attention to someone who has been to where you want to go or who has done what you wish to do, or who has succeeded in a venture of any kind in which you would also like to have success. When listening and taking direction, try to find out if the person giving the information has been successful before they started telling others how to do something. Your father is aware of crafty sales people who have learned the cunning art of deception with words to create an illusion of success. These types of people, as your father would say, could sell a refrigerator to an Eskimo. They are usually making money from the information they are giving rather than from telling you how they became successful *before* they started teaching. What were the principles, methods, ideas, and thinking that were done before success happened?

This is the major challenge when finding a mentor or a teacher. I have already demonstrated to you several fascinating moments. These have been truthful and honest, but it is up to you to decide if they are. The question for you is how do you verify the teacher? There are two parts to everyone, a physical presence and a non-physical presence. The non-physical part can be called your emotional guidance center. It is an energy which can discern what is truthful and what is not. It gives the physical you information on how you feel and it gives you your emotional state of mind. When you are feeling good and happy, this is usually a great indicator that what you are learning is beneficial to you. There is a phrase that I will give you which is, *always look for the golden nuggets*. This is a way of speaking which is called a metaphor. A metaphor is using words to describe something other than what the words themselves mean. They paint a picture of an idea. In this situation, it means there will be something positive and of value to learn or observe from whatever you are experiencing. This is the golden nugget that you are searching for, and it will be a reflection of your perception. You and only you can and will decide how you respond. This is one of the steps to mastery.

Even though I am a Silver Dragon using the word 'golden' implies something of greater value than silver does to most people. In the dragon world, there is no difference as each is of equal value.

After giving this lesson, Bry can tell that Ian's mind is full and he needs to do something fun and playful, so Bry makes a suggestion to his student. "Since we are at this beautiful lake, let's find some flat stones and skip them across the water. We can see who can get the most splashes and the furthest distance."

Ian thinks this a contest that he can easily win, so he is all in. He picks up a nicely shaped flat rock and sends it far out into the lake with many bounces.

He turns to Bry and says, "Okay my Silver Dragon friend, see if you can top that one. I don't see how because you are missing hands and arms to throw with."

"Well that is very true but you have forgotten about my tail." Bry walks over to the stones, finds one that he approves of, and with a nimble and delicate manipulation of his tail, snaps off a very powerful throw. Both of them laugh and each proceeds to toss more stones across the calm water.

It is an amazing day of learning and adventure. There are, however, two small companions that are also at the lake. W-L and Squeak, who followed Bry and Ian, and are on patrol. They are the first line of defense against any rodent invaders who may dare to attack the estate. Guardians must always be alert and ready for action. The whole of the estate may depend on their heroic actions. They are after all *The Great Defenders*.

Jim Dilyard lives in Wayne County Ohio. He is the owner of J D Producing, Inc. a producer of crude oil and natural gas which he has been doing for the last thirty-six years. He is a senior member of the Professional Bowlers Association and the 2010–2011 winner of the Pat Paterson award in the Central Region of the PBA. He is a two-time award winner for his writing at, *The Authors Show.com* and has co-authored a chapter in the book, **The Power of Imagination**, and appeared in the inspirational movie, **The Knowing**.